10/11

T 440 W9-CHR-027

Caroline Adderson

# Film Studies

Cass struggles to decide what role she should play in life, an act that swallows her whole. She's so cool she's cold. That's what people think, anyway. Her movie director father is always jet-setting somewhere exciting, as sophisticated as Cass herself wants to be.

Then along comes a hot new guy and a school film project—and things get strange. The green light on the web cam is glowing like a troll's eye, and Cass knows what's been captured. Is she still just a scared little nobody, or is it time to grow up?

**Single Voice**

1 book | 2 stories

## Also available in the Single Voice series

*Some mistakes can never been repaired*

### TRAIN WRECK
Malin Lindroth

The narrator of *Train Wreck* tells the story of the time she and her school friends played a trick on Susie P. The time Johnny—the narrator's *boyfriend* Johnny—got together with Susie P. But not for real. Except for Susie P., it was very real. She didn't see that everyone else was laughing. Johnny played with her, like a bored kid. Everyone agreed to go along. And then it went horribly wrong.

### TOO LATE
Clem Martini

What if you've done something so awful, your own mother doesn't even want you? The narrator in *Too Late* tells his parents he'll change, he'll be good, but they don't want him back. So he's stuck in a place with all the others who are out of options. Where does he head when there's nowhere left to run?

*Two heart-wrenching tales of sibling secrets, loyalty and loss*

### I AM NOT EMMANUELLE
Carine Tardieu

Thirteen-year-old Adele impulsively steals a pack of gum, launching her into a rambling monologue about her inability to live up to the "perfect" sister who died. Convinced that her parents would have preferred her to die instead, Adele can't help acting out.

### JUST JULIE
Nadia Xerri-L.

Julie's idolized older brother is accused of murder. When she refuses to attend his trial, her shattered family is bewildered. But Julie knows more about her brother than she wants to admit, and a fateful decision is in her hands: should she speak the truth, or protect her family?

Single Voice

Caroline Adderson

# Film
# Studies

 annick press
toronto + new york + vancouver

**Annick Press Ltd.**

Series editor: Melanie Little

Copyedited by Geri Rowlatt
Proofread by Tanya Trafford
Cover design by David Drummond/Salamander Hill Design
Interior design by Monica Charny
Cover photo (web camera) by zaharch / shutterstock.com

*For Shaena Lambert*

We acknowledge the support of the Canada Council for the Arts, the Ontario Arts Council, and the Government of Canada through the Canada Book Fund (CBF) for our publishing activities.

ONTARIO ARTS COUNCIL
CONSEIL DES ARTS DE L'ONTARIO

**Mixed Sources**
Product group from well-managed forests, controlled sources and recycled wood or fiber
**FSC** www.fsc.org Cert no. SW-COC-002358
© 1996 Forest Stewardship Council

Annick Press is committed to protecting our natural environment. As part of our efforts, the text of this book is printed on 100% post-consumer recycled fibers.

Printed and bound in Canada by Webcom.

Published in the U.S.A. by
Annick Press (U.S.) Ltd.

Distributed in Canada by
Firefly Books Ltd.
66 Leek Crescent
Richmond Hill, ON
L4B 1H1

Distributed in the U.S.A. by
Firefly Books (U.S.) Inc.
P.O. Box 1338
Ellicott Station
Buffalo, NY 14205

Visit our website at www.annickpress.com

There once was a girl who lay in bed for a long time every morning. In itself, this was hardly special. Most girls hate getting up. The alarm goes and they doze a bit, watching the light behind the curtains—is it raining or is it sunny?—until they figure out what to wear. But this girl was special. While she was drowsing in bed, she wasn't thinking about clothes. She was deciding which character to be that day. The Little

Match Girl frantically striking matches to keep herself from freezing to death? No, she didn't feel *that* pathetic. The Ugly Duckling? That only worked when she had a pimple or something, because she was half-Danish and the Danes are beautiful. The Snow Queen?

No. She's been the Snow Queen too much lately.

▬ •

Why do I do it? Why do I always need a role to play? My mother is, or was, an actress but I know I haven't inherited my dramatic tendencies from her. I'm not like

Aurora at all. I get them from Erlend, my father, who is a film director. But his being a director is only part of the reason. It's also because he started reading the tales of Hans Christian Andersen to me when I was a tiny baby in his arms. Later, after he left, Aurora read them to me. And then, when I could, I read them to myself.

I don't know who to be today. Maybe the princess in the "Princess and the Pea" because I've been sleeping so badly. But being a princess would involve a prince. No thanks. There is no prince in my life. I never consort with the opposite sex except in the case of Erlend, who breezes into town and makes a fuss over me once or twice a year. It's his fault I can't decide who I am this morning.

Because Erlend is here, in town, right now and he hasn't called me.

The curtains are burning white from the day behind them. The curtains are about to go up in flames, yet I just lie here feeling sick. Sick and undecided. Get up. Go, Cass. Go. So I do. I get up and get dressed, which is easy because I wear the same thing every day—jeans and a T-shirt with a man's white dress shirt thrown over it all, the white shirt showing off my blue eyes. Then I head for the kitchen and, despite the clothes I've just put on, I feel undressed,

I feel completely naked, for not knowing who to be.

I'm not hungry, but I should eat. Cereal flakes tinkle tinkle in the bowl. I don't want to wake Aurora, who is still in mourning, though it's been about a month.

Why does she do it? Over and over again, she chooses inappropriate men. I think it's because she's never really let go of Erlend. Who would—he's so gorgeous and accomplished. When he speaks, it's like he's singing to you. I lean right across the table, trying to hear every musical syllable he utters. In the candlelight, it feels like we're part of the night sky, like we're sitting in some flickering constellation instead of a restaurant. Erlend reaches for my hand and I know at that moment I'm the only one who matters to him. I am his personal star. He named me. Cassandra. "Cassandra. Tell me everything. What is happening in your life?"

That's what it's like to be with him, so I can imagine how it was seventeen years ago when he and Aurora first met. He had just come over from Denmark and was starting out with commercials. Aurora, too, was just starting out and had high hopes, but in the meantime she put on a lacy bra and twirled around for Erlend's camera. It was her fairy tale—to enchant a sophisticated older man. She enchanted him and then she had his child, who was me, and we all lived together for two years before the story soured. They were so poor and Erlend couldn't make the films he wanted and Aurora had to give up her dreams of being an actress and go to work in an insurance office. They fought all the time, she said, so he left and made a success of himself without us. She tells this story as often as she used to read Hans Christian Andersen to me.

The look on his face when he saw her for the first time. The lacy lightness as she twirled.

━━━ ●

"Tell me what is happening in your life."
He always asks. He e-mails, of course, but
just a few lines now and then, he's so busy
with his work. Birthdays and Christmases,
he sends clothes. Aurora hugs them to her
body, groans, "Oh, god! That I could fit
into this!" Because they are all beautiful.
Beautiful and expensive. He even buys me
underwear. I put his presents in a drawer
and only take them out to look at them. If
I wear them at all, it's when he comes to
town. I don't want to hurt his feelings.

At dinner, Erlend asked me what was
happening. "School's good," I told him.

"I'm taking Film Studies." I watched side-
long for his reaction, saw his silvery blond
eyebrows lift.

"That's an interesting choice. What does
one do in Film Studies?"

I laughed and pulled my hand out of his
so I could slap it. He teases me all the time
like this. "We're going to make a silent movie.
Well, a video. Can I tell you my idea?"

He leaned in, listening. When he's this
close, I'm always a little surprised by the
fact of his brown eyes. (The restaurant was
so dark I'd been half-imagining them as
blue, like mine.)

"It's supposed to be black and white. Two minutes long. So we need something simple. Remember that story 'The Snow Queen'? I want to make a film of that."

"The Snow Queen. The Snow Queen. Good."

He didn't remember. I could tell. "We're in groups of three and this one guy? Mason? I told him the story and he's into it. The other girl, not so much. But maybe she'll get sick or something."

The food arrived at our table, stacked in teetering piles, and Erlend smiled at me. "So. Film."

"Mason is going to direct. I'm going to act."

"Ah! Like your mother."

*Not* like my mother, I thought.

"You have her voice, too," Erlend said. "Deep. You sound older than you are."

Then we started talking about Aurora. Erlend is so polite. He always asks.

Last month I got up in the night and found the toilet full of amber pee, the seat up—for the last time, it turned out. Lionel and Aurora were finished, thank god. The contents of the toilet pretty much summed up Lionel as far as I was concerned, but there was no convincing Aurora at first. She went through the usual hell, dragging me along. I called in sick for her, spent hours convincing her she's still beautiful. I slept with her—sheets unwashed and smelling of Lionel's awful cologne, his *eau de toilette*. I ran the bath, undressed her, helped her into the tub. Her breasts hung down like empty socks—the woman who had once starred in a bra commercial! It was pathetic.

Me: "I never liked Lionel anyway."

Aurora said nothing.

"He left the seat up."

Aurora: "All men do. You'd better get used to it."

Me: "Untrue. Erlend puts the seat down, I bet. Also, Lionel went around in his underwear in front of me. I think that's inappropriate."

Aurora started to snivel, so I added something to soften my critique. "At least he wasn't married, like Charles."

"Charles wasn't married."

Me: "Right."

"He wasn't."

"Whatever."

"Why would you think he was married?"

"Because he only ever took you to lunch, never dinner. Because he wouldn't stay over."

"He didn't think it was *appropriate*. Because of you."

"Whatever."

I never told her about the phone call, about his wife shrieking things at me. She thought I was Aurora. She thought I was the one she was supposed to hate.

▬ ●

I never told Erlend either. Not about the phone call. Not about Lionel. I just said that Aurora had broken up with someone and was depressed about it. Erlend never mentions the women in his life, but I assume there are many, probably several at once, all of them beautiful actressy-types, which doesn't bother me, though I know that's hypocritical when I hated Charles for the very same thing. It's as though normal moral standards don't apply to Erlend.

By then we'd finished our main courses (mine, of course, toppled as soon as I touched it with my fork) and were looking at the dessert menu. Erlend always orders cheese, then makes me take little tastes of his. I prefer sweet things, frozen things. I chose *A selection of fresh fruit ices*.

"So this Mason?" he asked out of the blue. "Is he your boyfriend?"

I almost spat out my mouthful of ice. "No!"

The director smiled and said, "'The lady doth protest too much, methinks.'"

"Oh, Hamlet!" I said, in case he thought I didn't get the reference. Another little slap for him.

"So do you have a boyfriend?" he asked.

"No."

"I find that hard to believe," he said, "Is it a school for the blind that you go to?"

That's another thing about him that's so great. He flatters in unexpected ways. He doesn't just say you're pretty.

"Well, good," he said, touching the corners of his mouth with his napkin. "Then I don't have to be jealous."

But the best thing about that dinner was Erlend's news: he wasn't just passing through town this time. He was staying at least a month, shooting a film here. I thought of asking if I could come on set and watch him work, actually pictured my own canvas chair with *Director's Daughter* printed on the back. Maybe I could get some credit for it at school.

But what I really hoped was that there might be a part for me. A small part. I could be an extra.

I didn't ask, though. He's very private about his work. Also, I was sort of speechless about him being around for a whole month. When he put me in the cab, he said he would call in a few days. I'd ask him then.

But he hasn't called. That dinner was two weeks ago and he hasn't called me yet.

▬▬●

The cereal crackles in the blue bowl like stepped-on glass. Like ice. I carry it to the table. Quiet, quiet. Don't wake Aurora up. She seems a bit better this week. She's taking care of herself again, putting on her colored scarves and bangles and outlining her sad blue eyes in black. I don't have to lie now when I say she's still beautiful. She's back at work (she has Fridays off, which is why she's home today catching up on all the sleep she's missed). This is just like us. We're never happy at the same time.

The blue bowl is my favorite, the color of

the Danish sky I've never seen. I uncap the
milk and slosh some in. Poor me. Poor me,
waiting for Erlend. I was too young when
he left us to remember it. But now I can
imagine how Aurora felt. It must have been
Lionel times ten. Lionel *and* Charles put
together, squared, then times ten. It must
have been like how I feel now.

Like I'm an extra, not a star at all.

I'm an extra in my father's life.

━━ ●

At school, a lot of boys like me. I know
they do. They follow me with their eyes as

I walk the halls in my big boots. My over-sized white shirt flaps behind me like swan wings. They don't approach me. They think I'm stuck up, a princess, but what would I ever see in a sixteen-year-old boy? They're so crude. They think everything is funny—burping, farting, throwing up. Sex. I don't find those things funny. Not at all. Not one bit.

I'd never seen Mason before I signed up for Film Studies because he's new to our school. First I noticed his melting smile, then how smart he seemed. Most kids take Film Studies because they want to watch movies during school or make stupid little videos on their phones. They can't believe they have to sit through the whole history of film, starting with the oldest ones, which are in black and white and don't even have sound. All over the darkened room, heads lolled on desks. But Mason's stayed upright, with his crazy hair flaring around it. The two of us were probably the only ones awake.

After class he waited. He wasn't afraid to talk to me. "I hear you're Danish."

"Half," I corrected. I knew where he'd heard it, from Jerrilyn, or someone in her clique. Once I mentioned it in class and ever since she's taunted me with it, having nothing to be proud of herself. She's nothing.

Mason said, "I'm half something too."

"Half what?" I asked, curious.

"Half the opposite of you. My mother's from Barbados." Which was why he looked so tanned and his hair was so crazy and why the sun shines out of his face.

"It's my father who's Danish," I told him.

During class, Mason's hand kept going up as he asked and answered practically every question. He already knew about Eadweard Muybridge and his galloping horse. He'd already seen the film for that day, Georges Méliès's *A Trip to the Moon*. (Even though it was made in 1902, he'd seen it!) So I guess I wanted him to know that other people knew things too when I added, "My father's a director."

"A director?" he said. "No way. What kind of films does he make?"

And I felt so embarrassed. Because I've never actually seen Erlend's films. When I was younger, he told me his work was un-suitable for children. Eventually I stopped asking. "They're pretty arty," I told Mason, "and difficult to understand."

He shrugged that off. "Are they subtitled or in English?"

Even that made me pause. "Some are,"

I told him.

"What?" he asked.

"Both."

"I'll look them up," he said, and I was doubly embarrassed then because it's something I've never bothered to do. I guess I always thought I would watch them with Erlend. When Erlend thought I was ready for them.

"Wow," he said as we headed off in different directions. "A director's daughter. *That's so cool.*"

▬▬ ●

Cool. That's what they always say about me.
I'm so cool I'm cold. The cereal crackles,
the milk sloshes, then I hear another
sound. A low gravelly laugh coming from
behind the closed bedroom door just off
the kitchen. From Aurora's room.

And I set the milk down, unquietly.

That's not Aurora's laugh. She laughs like
she cries, loud enough for the whole building
to know her sorrows and her joys. In other
words, she's a bad actress.

There is a man in my mother's bedroom.
Another one. I have no idea where she met
him. In some lame singles' chat room? At

work? Sometimes I heard her at night with Lionel, just like I heard her with all the others. Except Charles, who, I guess, took her to his office. It was horrible. I didn't want to listen.

I wanted to turn the sound off.

I remember that phone call last year. Lifting the receiver, offering my innocent "Hello." A strange rasping breath on the other end. It was so creepy I would have hung up except I realized the person on the other end was crying. "Who is this? Are you okay?"

"Who do you think it is?" she sobbed.

"I don't know."

"No? I think you do."

"I really don't."

"Well, I know who you are," she said.
I thought it was a wrong number. I didn't
get it until she said, "Actually, I know *what*
you are. A slut! You're a slut!"

I hung up, but for a long time, I stood
trembling by the phone, in case it rang
again and Aurora answered.

━━ •

At the start of "The Snow Queen," an evil troll gets his hands on a strange mirror. In it, everything beautiful shrinks to nothing and everything ugly becomes even more grotesque. A single pimple would spread across your face like fungus. He and the other evil trolls ran all over the world with it until there wasn't a person who hadn't been distorted in its glass. They still weren't finished, though—they decided to fly up to heaven to make more trouble there. On the way, one of them dropped the mirror and it fell back to Earth, where it smashed into a billion pieces. But because each tiny fragment retained its distorting properties, whenever a speck got into someone's eye, that person would only see what was bad about a thing. Their eyes would turn cold and critical. Some people even got a splinter in their hearts and, when that happened, it was practically incurable. Their heart became a lump of ice.

━━ •

They were quiet last night, but now I deliberately make noise. I play on the bowl with the spoon. Ding, ding, ding, ding, ding… How about some orange juice? I get up for the carton, slam the fridge. Slam the carton down on the counter. Slam the cupboard when I take down a glass. Slam the glass. Hey, I'm so musical!

> *Ding, ding, SLAM!*
> *Ding, ding, SLAM!*
> *Ding, ding, SLAM!*

Maybe Aurora thinks I'm mad, thinks it's why I'm bashing everything like this. But I'm not. I don't care if she wants to plunge back into another rotten fairy tale. I just want them to know I'm awake and up. I just want them to stay in bed until I've left for school so I don't have to meet the new guy.

There. I've made enough noise to wake the building, but it's as if they don't even hear. Aurora's laughing, too loudly. Ha ha ha ha!

Oh, shut up.

Most people change their outfit every day, but some don't. I don't.

I can be the Snow Queen again.

━━ ●

Mason hung around after our second Film Studies class, but I walked right past him. I didn't want him to think I was interested. Now and then I would catch sight of him in the hall between classes. Every time, I looked the other way.

Later in the week, he came up to me at my

locker when I was taking out my books. I couldn't ignore him because my hands were full, my combination lock dangling open. He seemed about to say something, but then he didn't. He did the strangest thing instead. He pursed his lips and blew a stream of warm air into my face. He blew on me, then turned and walked away while I stood staring after him, wondering what it meant.

His breath smelled sweet, like fruit.

It must have been his gum.

We were supposed to get into groups of

three for our first project. I saw Mason had
paired up with Jerrilyn. Jerrilyn has blonde
hair, too, but it's bleached. She has a daisy
tattooed on the small of her back. She
kept dropping her pencil so she could
bend over and pick it up off the floor.
Every time, the daisy bloomed in the space
of skin between her short top and her low-
rise jeans. This was for Mason's benefit, I
presumed. I saw him look at it. I saw him
look at that flower and I went over and
asked, "Can I be in your group?"

Jerrilyn shot me a glance. (And they say
*I'm* cold!) Mason smiled and pulled a chair
up for me.

We brainstormed our ideas. Mine was the story. "A little boy and girl live across from each other on a rooftop. They love each other like brother and sister. One day, during a snowstorm, the boy's grandmother tells them about the Snow Queen. The next day the Queen appears to the little boy and steals him away." We would have to do just a part of the story. Obviously. The film was only supposed to be two minutes long.

"Where are we going to get a little boy?" asked Jerrilyn, sneerily.

"We could steal one," Mason said.

I suggested the Snow Queen steal a baby

instead. A doll. Jerrilyn said it was a dumb idea, but Mason liked it. He said that Georges Méliès made films of fairy tales.

"Who's Georges Méliès?" Jerrilyn asked.

━━ ●

Now Aurora and her new conquest are stirring in the bedroom. I hear rustling as clothes, thrown off in a hurry last night, are picked up off the floor and put back on. More laughter. Quick, get out. I take my dishes to the sink and drop them in with a clatter. Turn the tap on high, squirt in way, way too much soap.

We shot the film in Mason's back yard last
Saturday night because no one was home.
Jerrilyn was in charge of costumes and
props. A white nightie, snow spray. Two
feather pillows. A baby carriage and a doll.
I walked through the garden, barefoot in
the nightie, like a sleepwalker. Frost settled
on everything I passed. (Talcum powder.)
When I reached the baby carriage and
lifted out the child, snow began to fall.
(Jerrilyn in a tree, letting go handfuls of
feathers.)

It hardly ever snows here, not more than
once or twice a winter. Once, when it did,
I ran out into the garden in my underwear
just to feel the thousand tiny flakes touching

down on my bare skin. They scorched and tingled as they melted. Cooling trickles running down my bare legs. I thought of that while Mason filmed me.

"Cut!" he called.

Then we went inside to watch it on his computer. It had seemed so hokey acting it out in the yard, but on the screen it wasn't too bad, mostly because of how Mason had worked the camera and set up the lights. He had an editing program on his computer and would fix it up later by cutting in other footage, stuff like that.

Jerrilyn had to go. "Can I get my nightie

back?" she asked me.

I changed back into my clothes. After Jerrilyn left, it was just the two of us, me and
Mason. "Do you want a beer?" he asked.
We drank it in his room and, while we
were talking, Mason brought up Erlend
again. "You've never even *asked* about his
films?"

I told him what Erlend said to me when I
was little. "He said I wouldn't like them.
He said I was too young to understand
them."

"But you're not a kid anymore. You're
sixteen. You must be curious. You signed

up for Film Studies."

That bothered me a lot—I felt he was accusing me of being immature. "I guess I'm not as much of a cinephile as you," I said, snarky, not that Mason even noticed. He just smiled and said, "I bet it's porn. They make a lot of porn in Scandinavia."

I wondered, had he looked Erlend up? And did I really want to know what kind of films my father makes?

━━ ●

A snowdrift of bubbles is mounting in the sink. The pile grows and grows and some of the bubbles break free and become airborne. They float up, up, then slowly drift back down. It's snowing in the kitchen, huge clumped flakes of soap. One clump keeps growing, gets bigger and bigger until it becomes a woman dressed in a gauzy gown woven out of millions of tiny, star-like flakes. She is beautiful and delicate, but she is made of ice—glaring, glittering ice.

I am furious.

I'll confront Erlend, I decide as I wash my bowl. When he calls me, I'll ask why he took so long. I'll ask why I mean so little to him that he can ignore me. And I'll ask to see one of his films. Why shouldn't I, now that I've made one too?

Mason and I talked about what we could cut into our version of "The Snow Queen."

"We'll have to do more shooting," he said.

"When?" I asked.

"How about right now?" Mason said and he kissed me with his hot, fruity mouth. I felt entranced, shivering and tingling all over, like in the garden. It scared me, that feeling, but I wanted it. I wanted to feel it and I wanted it to last and not just be a memory that would melt away.

The soapy water pours out of the sink and

sloshes over my bare feet. The lace camisole and panties that Erlend bought me, why else had I worn them? I knew something would happen. Mason didn't trick me. In fact, it was partly my idea.

And I drop the blue bowl on the floor, where it smashes. It smashes to pieces and Erlend hasn't phoned in two weeks. Two weeks! Today I feel like Aurora—dumped, rejected, bereft. There has to be a pea under my futon, I've been sleeping so badly since that night at Mason's. I can't eat. Before I dropped the bowl and broke it, I threw half my cereal down the sink.

Water is overflowing the sink now, pouring

down the cupboard door, pooling around my bare feet. Pieces of the shattered bowl lie everywhere. Then the bedroom door opens and I swing around and there he is. Like in a fairy tale, I've conjured Erlend just by wishing so hard for him. He looks different unshaven, but the smile is the same. I rush to him but my feet hit the soapy water and fly out from under me and I crash down hard on the floor and the dangerous shards of the broken bowl. Then I'm wailing because it hurts. It hurts to have to wait and wait.

Erlend comes over and kneels beside me and gathers me, wet and shaking, in his arms. I must be dreaming him, but he feels real.

"Cassandra," he murmurs. "Poor Cassandra."

"The tap!" says Aurora, coming out of the bedroom and hurrying to turn it off before the whole kitchen floods. "What's going on?"

And I freeze like the Little Match Girl, stiff in Erlend's arms. They see my surprise and, exchanging a look, both of them laugh. In the middle of this mess, with me sobbing, they *laugh*? Aurora is only now doing up the sash of her robe. Obviously they thought I'd be delighted to find them together like this. My parents? Are they insane? Erlend left her. He already left her once.

"Are you okay, sweetheart?" Aurora asks as

I push away from Erlend and scramble to
my feet. "Stay. Sit with us while we have
coffee," she says. "You can be late."

"*Why didn't you call me?*" I scream at Erlend.

━━━ ●

"Turn around," I said, and Mason did.
Then I took off my white man's shirt and
my T-shirt and sat shivering in my
camisole. "Okay," I said.

Mason turned back and, with the video
camera to his eye, it was easier. I didn't feel
so shy. I'd been sitting on the edge of his
bed, but now I stood.

"What about your jeans?" he asked.

I undid my belt and stepped out of them. Then I stood on the bed. I stood on the bed dressed in those lacy bits of silk and I felt very cold. Freezing. I began to turn and Mason started moving around me, getting down low with the camera. I am pale and lacy, twirling in the dark. Erlend once made a bra commercial. What kind of films does he make now, Erlend who is exempt from normal moral standards?

I was acting in one. I was acting this part for Erlend.

See? I can be anyone I want.

And I get so dizzy that I fall. That, too, Mason films. Me falling on the bed and my hair flying out and my cold arms reaching for him.

━━ •

Aurora knocks on my bedroom door, but I tell her to go away. I shout, "I won't help you this time! When *he* leaves? You're on your own! Do you hear me?"

"Cass?" she pleads through the door.

I remember that phone call and take those same ugly words that shocked me so much and throw them at her. "You're a slut!

You're just a slut! Leave me alone!"

On my bed, I sob. Everything hurts where I went down—knees, elbows, the heels of my hands—it all throbs. It's a miracle I'm not cut. I'm going to be covered in bruises tomorrow, but that's the least of the pain I feel. Erlend and Aurora are whispering in the kitchen. I hear little whimpers, too—I've made my mother cry again. Erlend's soothing tone. He's comforting her. But what about me? What about me?

Another knock. "Cassandra?" he says, like a bird calling in a tree. "Ca-san-dra? May I come in?" And he doesn't wait for my permission but comes in and shuts the door softly behind him. He sits on the edge of the bed. "I did call," he finally says.

"When?"

"A few days later, like I said I would."

I sit up. "She never told me! She never gave me the message! I hate her! I hate her so much!"

Erlend winces when I say this, like I'm talking about hating him. "Cassandra," he says, "don't say that. It's not her fault. Truthfully? I may not have left a message for you."

"What do you mean?"

"I called for you, yes. But you weren't in.
Aurora and I started talking. The first real
talk we've had in years. You told me those
things she was going through. It's been
difficult for her. I haven't been here for her.
Not for you either. I did mean to call you
again, but I got so busy with the shoot."

"You had time for Aurora!" I point out.
He looks embarrassed. "Yes. I took her to
dinner last night."

Oh, I see it all now. Erlend saying, "Aurora,
tell me what is happening in your life,"
and Aurora counting out on her painted
fingertips all the princes who have failed
her. Making herself pathetic to win his
sympathy.

Erlend smiles. "Should I have asked your permission?"

"She could have told me!"

"I'm sure she was going to," he says. "She hasn't had the chance."

And then my father says something that surprises me very much. He says, "Cassandra, I'm lonely."

He sounds like a child when he says it, and I feel childish, too, for the things I've said. But I'm not a child. I'm not a child anymore. Far from it. And Erlend? He's just disgusting. It's sick to make films like that. I blurt it out, "What kind of films are you making that you can't show them to your own daughter?"

He's taken aback, wondering where this outburst came from. "What?" he asks.

"Why haven't you ever shown me your films?"

I can see he feels caught. He starts looking everywhere but at me. "You wouldn't be interested, Cassandra."

"I am! I'm very interested. So why can't you show them to me?"

"Why are you asking me now? Oh, it's

because of Film Studies. Is that it?"

"Don't put me off! You're always putting me off! I've asked so many times!"

"When?"

"Before!" I shout, which, I realize, was probably eight or nine years ago.

He smiles and takes me in his arms. I try to struggle free, but he won't let me. He locks me in and tells me how much he loves me. "Who's my little girl? Who's my Cassie?" His embarrassing name for me once upon a time. "I have some demos. I might even have some in my bag. I'll leave them for you. I worry what you'll think, though, Cass. That you'll think less of me. Nothing turned out the way I planned. With my career, I mean."

It's so creepy and sick to think of watching those films. I can't even speak, I'm so appalled, but then Erlend laughs and I'm his child again. The one he used to read fairy tales to.

But I'm too old for fairy tales now. Much too old.

When I finally come out of my room, I've

already missed my first class. Erlend is gone. Only Aurora is there, on her hands and knees with a rag in her hand, sopping up the last of the puddle on the floor. I see all the broken pieces of my favorite bowl lined up on the counter. Does she actually plan on gluing them back together?

Aurora gets up off the floor, wrings the rag out in the sink, offers me a timid smile. I toss my head.

"You're not jealous, are you?" she asks.

I scoff—loudly.

Then she says something really sad. She says, "There's no reason to be, Cass. It won't last."

I ignore her and go to get my backpack off the hook by the door. But as I'm reaching up for it, I glance back at her on her hands and knees again. I can see down her bathrobe to her shabby, discolored bra. It was awful what I said to her. And one of my eyes starts to tear up. It's weird because I've just bawled my head off. You'd think anything stuck in my eye would already have washed out, but here I am, gushing on one side, the eye burning and stinging. I forget about the backpack and, blinking madly, hurry into the bathroom.

The seat is up, the water yellow with pee. I turn away in disgust. In the mirror, I pull down my lower lid.

Aurora stands in the doorway. "What's the matter?"

"I've got something in my eye."

"Let me see," she says, and I tilt my head back and let her look. "Is it an eyelash?" she asks.

"I don't know."

I'm starting to feel a bit hysterical, thinking it might be glass in my eye from the broken bowl. Aurora is so close to me I can see her pores and freckles through my tears, see how, without makeup, all her suffering shows. She turns on the tap, lets the water run cold. "Wash it," she says, and I bend

my head, scooping the water in my cupped
palm, splashing the eye that hurts. While
I'm doing this, Aurora keeps one hand on
my back. I feel the warmth of it radiating
across my shoulder blades and down my
spine. I straighten with eyes squeezed shut
and when I open them again, we are together,
framed in the mirror, heads together, my
blue eyes soothed and blinking, Aurora's,
the identical color, filled with concern.

"Better?" she asks.

"Yes," I say.

Then she hugs me and I let her. I let her
because the one thing I can't do is tell her

I'm sorry for what I said. The words won't
form in my mouth. After a minute, I pull
back and say, "Look."

Aurora turns, sees the toilet seat up,
laughs. "I told you! They're all the same."

She starts walking me back to the door,
but in the hall she remembers and says,
"Oh, Cass. Erlend left something for you."

━━ •

I said to Mason, "Shut the camera off."

"Okay," he said and set it on his desk next
to his computer. By then we had both

drunk three beers. My head was spinning, the bed was spinning. I felt very cold. I'm always cold. But then Mason crawled into the bed next to me and put his hot arms around me and I felt myself melting, melting into him.

"Take your shirt off," I said. I wanted to feel the heat from his skin.

He tossed it on the floor.

"What about your jeans?" I said.

He looked a little afraid. Afraid and amazed, yet he got up and did exactly what I said. Then he was standing in front of me, the hottest boy in our school, naked

and shivering. Who would ever guess that
I would be the one to warm him up?
Did I do it for Erlend or for Mason?

I don't know. I just don't know.

When we finished, I sat up and put my
clothes on, sick about what I'd done. I
didn't bother with the pretty camisole, just
stuffed it in the back pocket of my jeans. I
pulled on my T-shirt, my socks and boots.
I felt hideous and wondered, is there a story
like "The Ugly Duckling" but in reverse?

Mason sat up and said, "Do you like me?"

"Shh," I said.

"You're beautiful. Don't go all cold on me.
You can't ask me to do this and then just
walk out."

"Do we have to talk?" I asked.

"Cass? What about at school?"

I turned and looked at him sitting on the
bed. Then I looked at the computer on the
desk and saw what I knew I would see,
Mason on the screen, talking to me, asking
me not to go.

And I saw the green lights on either side
of the web cam, glowing like a little pair of
troll's eyes. The video camera was off, but
the computer had filmed everything.

"Cass."

I didn't answer because it was a silent movie. None of the sounds we made would ever be heard. And because the whole room had filled with snow. A blizzard was raging through the house. A white-out. I wrapped my gauze around me and vanished into it.

━━━ •

Aurora comes back with a couple of DVDs in her hand. "He's coming on Saturday. Is that alright? Can we have dinner together? The three of us?" She hands me the disks. "I don't know why he thinks you'd be interested in these."

"What do you mean?" I ask.

Aurora shrugs. "Industrial films?"

I don't understand. She must see it on my face because she holds them up and reads the labels out to me. "*Boiler Room Safety— It's Easier Than You Think. New Procedures in Baggage Handling—*"

"He makes industrial films?" I interrupt.

She blinks at me. "You knew that, Cass."

"No," I say. "I didn't."

She shakes her head, her voice full of pity. "Poor Erlend. He wanted to be an *auteur,* the next Lars von Trier or something, but there's no money in that. I thought you knew the kind of films he made. I thought it would have come up during one of your romantic dinners. Are you disappointed?" She looks at me hard, like she wants me to be disappointed in Erlend instead of her, for once.

I can't tell her. I can't explain that the only thing that comes close to the shame and embarrassment of finding out your father makes porn is finding out that he doesn't.

━━ ●

All week I've been avoiding Mason, but he

keeps trying to talk to me. He keeps saying, "I won't show it to anyone. I'll erase it if you tell me to."

Second period. Film Studies. I slide into the desk next to his in the dark. Another black and white film. It has sound this time, but seems to be in a foreign language. Everyone else is asleep.

I lean into Mason and finally, finally I speak.

I say, "I want to see it."

●

Billie Livingston

# The Trouble with Marlene

Sixteen-year-old Samantha is miserable. They used to be a family—Sammie, her father, and her mother, Marlene. Back then they were hustlers, living off the misery of others. But now Marlene is alone and completely off the rails, spending her days drinking red wine and dreaming up the perfect suicide.

No one at school has any idea what Sammie's world is like. No one but Drew, and Sammie's not sure she wants to let him in. Sitting on the edge of Marlene's bed, she wonders if Marlene might be right after all. What's so great about this life, anyway?

## Also available in the Single Voice series

*Friendship confronts authority in these raw, powerful stories*

### DESCENT INTO PARADISE
Vincent Karle

When the new kid from Afghanistan is put in Martin's class, Martin ridicules his clothes and nicknames him "Taliban." But the two realize they have more in common than they thought, and unexpectedly become friends—until a brutal drug bust at school tears them apart ... maybe forever.

### A PLACE TO LIVE
Jean-Philippe Blondel

Some people might think it's odd when a teenage boy starts making movies of his classmates kissing. But in *A Place to Live*, the aspiring filmmaker's project turns into a compelling protest against authoritarianism that could get him kicked out of school, and expose his own surprising feelings.

*Two fearless explorations of the depths
of teenage passion*

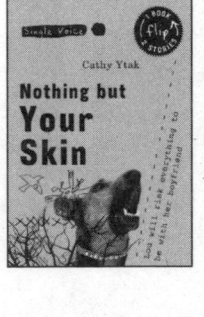

## NOTHING BUT YOUR SKIN
### Cathy Ytak

Louella hates her name. She's obsessed with colors and when she gets upset, she yells herself hoarse. People call her "slow," but Lou knows one thing for sure: she wants to be with her boyfriend—no matter what her parents or doctors think. *Nothing But Your Skin* chronicles the aftermath of a mentally challenged girl's decision to have sex.

## THE POOL WAS EMPTY
### Gilles Abier

Sixteen-year-old Celia's boyfriend, Alex, is dead after falling into an empty swimming pool—and his mother has accused Celia of his murder. As Celia tries to clear her name and move on from her devastating loss, she reveals that the shocking events of that fateful day may not be what they seem.

Single Voice

Billie Livingston

# The
# Trouble
## with Marlene

annick press
toronto + new york + vancouver

**Annick Press Ltd.**

Series editor: Melanie Little

Copyedited by Geri Rowlatt
Proofread by Tanya Trafford
Cover design and photo (broken glass) by
   David Drummond / Salamander Hill Design
Interior design by Monica Charny

We acknowledge the support of the Canada Council for the Arts, the Ontario Arts Council, and the Government of Canada through the Canada Book Fund (CBF) for our publishing activities.

ONTARIO ARTS COUNCIL
CONSEIL DES ARTS DE L'ONTARIO

**Cataloging in Publication**

Adderson, Caroline, 1963-
   Film studies / Caroline Adderson.

(Single voice series)
Title on added t.p., inverted: The trouble with Marlene / Billie
   Livingston.
ISBN 978-1-55451-261-4 (bound).—ISBN 978-1-55451-260-7 (pbk.)

I. Livingston, Billie, 1965- . II. Livingston, Billie, 1965- . Trouble
With Marlene. III. Title. IV. Series: Single voice series

PS8551.D3267F54 2010          jC813'.54          C2010-901764-1


| Published in the U.S.A. by | Distributed in Canada by | Distributed in the U.S.A. by |
|---|---|---|
| Annick Press (U.S.) Ltd. | Firefly Books Ltd. | Firefly Books (U.S.) Inc. |
| | 66 Leek Crescent | P.O. Box 1338 |
| | Richmond Hill, ON | Ellicott Station |
| | L4B 1H1 | Buffalo, NY 14205 |

**Visit our website at www.annickpress.com**

I used to lie awake till two or three in the morning and think of the easiest ways to die: eating Drano (in gel capsules so it'd just slip down), electrocution (blow-dryer in the bathtub), fast-moving truck (stepping in front of). On a talk show I saw a few months back, a woman told about how her son died by autoerotic asphyxiation. He hanged himself with a necktie in his closet, accidentally suffocating while he

jerked off over a porno mag. I wouldn't
need any of that, just the tie.

I probably sound like a major psycho.
Maybe I am. But if I am then it runs in
the family. My mom thinks about killing
herself all the time lately. Except Marlene
thinks it out loud. It's crazy. She used to
be so cool—and I was her kid so I felt like
it rubbed off on me in a way. Not so long
ago, it was her and me against the world.
Now look at us: a pair of defectives. How
did we get this way?

It's Sam's fault, the way I figure it. If my
dad hadn't screwed up, he wouldn't have
landed in jail and they never would have

split up. And if my parents hadn't split up, we wouldn't have been so broke and if we hadn't been broke Marlene never would have tried the bullshit con-job that sent her off the rails in the first place.

I am sitting on the edge of Marlene's bed, watching her breathe. Watching her gives me a weird buzz in my guts, like a bee in a jar.

One night a couple of weeks ago, my mother was on the couch, putting on her makeup because she was going to go drown herself. She was going to throw

herself off a pier, she said, and then she put more lipstick on. Marlene likes the idea of looking pretty when she dies. So she kept at it, putting on layer after layer of mascara while she talked about how she would dive off into the ocean. "My bones drifting free, finally free," she said, all dreamy, as if it was the most beautiful thing ever.

In other words, I thought, you want to be a jellyfish, one of those floating, white ballerina-things that dance in the quietest parts of the water. Not me. My death would be final—just one step off the curb at rush hour.

She caught me rolling my eyes.

"You know *everything*, don't you?" She took another slug of her vodka and milk, zipped up her makeup bag, and announced she was going to jump off the roof of our building instead.

I didn't say anything.

"So superior…" she sputtered. "I was going to get you a nice little bottle of sparkling wine for your sweet sixteenth! But you'd have turned your nose up at *that*!"

"My body is a temple," I said.

"Oh for chrissake! Why couldn't you just turn Catholic like a normal person?"

It's because of Marlene that I even *know*
any born-again-Christian kids. She had
the bright idea to send me to summer camp
a couple of years ago so she and Fat Freddy
could take off for a week and work a few
hustles in Los Angeles. It turned out to be
one of those Jesus camps. The Welfare
paid for it. Most of the camps Welfare pays
for are Jesus camps. It's like they think that
poor kids must all be morally bankrupt, too.

So my best friend is a born-again. Drew
goes to the same high school as me. He's
not super pious or anything, just kind of
abnormally clean-living. Which suits me
fine because I'm abnormal, too. If I were
normal, I wouldn't be a virgin who doesn't

drink or smoke. But I'm not like Marlene, and I'm not going to be. Which really gets on her nerves. And it makes me an outcast as far as almost everyone at school is concerned. All they want to do is party and get drunk and stoned. Like Marlene. What they don't get is, if you act like Marlene, you end up like Marlene. Messed up and lonely and broke.

Who else will have me but Drew? He *likes* it that I'm a freak. He's taken me to some of those church group youth functions. *Treat your body as a temple*, the youth pastor says. That one drives Marlene bats. "Holier than thou sons-of-bitches," she says.

It pisses me off when she slags all that religious stuff as being totally not like us—I suppose because I'm scared she's right. I mean, why *is* Drew friends with me? Maybe he's only nice to me because he *has* to be, has to turn his other cheek—it's in the Bible. Meanwhile, I don't know if I even believe in God. If I did, would I still sit around thinking about how long it would take to suffocate with a dry-cleaning bag tied over my head? At the Jesus camp, they sang this song that went *I've got the joy joy joy down in my heart.* I don't think I have that. Neither does my mother.

From the corner of my eye, I could see Marlene turn around on the couch and

stare at me. "I love you, you know," she said. "More than anything in the world."

I wanted to pound her for that.

"How're you going to get on the roof?" I asked her, in this very matter-of-fact way.

She blinked. "Fine. I'll go up to the top floor and jump off someone's balcony." As though neither of us mattered. Then she pulled her purse straps over her shoulder, stood up, and went strutting down the hallway like it was a red carpet.

"Yeah?" I got up and followed her. "Who'd let *you* in?"

"That won't be hard." She opened the

front door and tossed me a creepy starlet glance over her shoulder. "I'll just smile." Her teeth flashed.

I watched her head down the hall and push the elevator button. She waved to me as she got on. I slammed the apartment door.

*Do it then. See if I care.* Part of me wished she would, too. I wondered what it would sound like, her soft body hitting the pavement.

I wandered into Marlene's room. The top drawer in her dresser was open—that's where she keeps her stash. I plucked out a prescription bottle: Valium 10 mg. When I turned it over, all the little blue happy pills

rattled around. Actually, "happy pills" is a misnomer. They're "I-don't-give-a-crap pills." She'd recently become a big fan of Ativan, too. Same thing.

I read once about this woman who took Valium before she cut her wrists and then bled to death in a nice hot bath. Does blood look beautiful when you're stoned on Valium? In the dresser mirror, my pupils looked like holes in my head. Little black monsters stared out of them. I pushed my hair back out of my face. All the hot girls at school seem to have sleek TV hair; mine is a frizzy, curly, snaky mess. The first time I talked to Drew, he said, "Man, I love your hair—it's that wild

witchy hippie kinda hair." He *loved* it, he said. I started to not mind my head so much after that. Drew likes when I wear black, drapey hippie blouses, too. I have lots of those now.

I don't know how long I stood there thinking about that stuff, but suddenly the front door opened and Marlene came waltzing in, all giddy and grinning. I dropped the Valium back in her drawer. Turned out she'd been hanging out with the goof upstairs, the unemployed guy with the mustache who lies around on his balcony all day, tanning. I went to my bedroom and closed the door.

━━ ●

The only thing worse than Marlene being home is waiting for Marlene to come home. Last week, I came in from school and she wasn't there. No note. I knew she was probably out drinking some place where there were guys. It was two in the morning when she finally showed up.

I heard her before I saw her. She was out back with some jerk. My mother has the worst taste in men you ever saw in your life.

"Come on, Jack, just for a minute," she kept saying. Her S's were sliding all over the place. The guy's voice was too low to make out. Marlene got louder. "Look at me, Jack, please?" Right outside my bedroom

window. Made me sick to hear her beg like that. I pulled the pillow over my head.

Suddenly, clippy footsteps came down the little cement path beside our balcony. And then the Romanian accent of Nadia, the caretaker's wife.

"Marlene!" she said in a loud whisper. "You are waking up half the building."

I wondered why it was Nadia and not her husband, George, coming out in the middle of the night. Seems like Nadia always does the dirty work.

"This is *my* goddamn place," my mother said to Nadia, "and I'll do whatever the hell I like."

I peered through the crack between the curtains. I saw parts of Nadia—short, choppy hair, pajama pants, and her elbow jumping around in a woolly sweater.

"Get inside your goddamn place," Nadia hissed, "or I will call the police!"

Then the jerk spoke up. "Let's calm down."

"Don't tell me what to do!" That was Marlene talking, of course.

I listened until our apartment door opened and closed. There was scuffling and bumping, my mother saying, *Oops*, and giggling.

I tried to let my brain fade into sleep. After a while, my mom's voice came high and needy again, like a baby, like a Siamese cat. "I love you, Jack. I *love* you."

That was the capper.

"I never even said *I love you* to your father," Marlene once told me. "Only you. The second you were born I loved you."

Meanwhile, I'd never even heard of Jack.

I opened my bedroom door and stood there, looking into the living room, where my mother was on the couch pawing the guy's face. Jack was all leathery brown and skinny, like a science project. I swear to

god, he was like one of those bog men who gets preserved in peat for a hundred years.

"Mom!"

She jerked around. "Sammie." Her voice went all honey-pie. "Come here." She patted the bit of empty couch beside her. "Jack, this is my little girl."

"Hello," the bog man said. Long, bony fingers wriggled the air toward me. "You want to keep it down? I have to sleep. I've got school."

Marlene often says it's my tone that pisses her off, not the words. She slapped my face once last year for my tone. I looked at

her with this hard, amused expression that I'd been working on, and she ran like hell into her bedroom, slamming the door. I could hear her dresser drawer rattle as she rooted around for something that would take the edge off.

Now, her mouth hung open for a good three seconds before she blurted, "You slept *last* night. You're *always* sleeping."

"Are you for real?" I went back to my room and closed the door. Leaning against it, I listened as Jack made noises about leaving. Marlene told him she loved him again. Jack left.

I didn't speak to her the next morning. She didn't notice; she was sleeping.

After school that day, I could see Nadia outside our apartment door as I came down the hallway. Her voice was sharp and hacking, and she was jabbing a finger at Marlene.

My mother kept her arms folded.

Nadia's expression changed into a smile for me. I tried to make nice as I slipped past her to my mother's side of the door.

As soon as I was by her, Nadia went back to that harsh sneer. "You think you can wake up half the building and nothing is going to happen? Not so!"

"Where's George? When I signed the rental agreement for this godforsaken hole, I signed it for *George*." Marlene figures a guy will always treat you better. She'll go to the longest line in the supermarket just to deal with a guy.

"*George*! George has *had* it with you. He'd have kicked you out a long time ago but he likes Samantha. He thinks she's cute. Lucky for you."

Marlene's mouth hardened. "That *is* lucky," she said. If she'd been a cat, her tail would have been switching, hard.

My lungs clenched.

"If I have to speak to you again, no more chances!" Nadia gave me another gruesome smile before she hurried away, her tough little legs zipping down the hallway.

I made a beeline for my room.

Marlene followed me. "*George thinks Sammie's cute!* Isn't she cute with those trashy tight jeans painted on her teenaged ass? Cutest thing you ever saw." Then she stormed into the kitchen and slammed things around in the sink. "Maybe cute Sammie should haul her cute ass out here and clean up the kitchen!"

I am sitting on the edge of Marlene's bed now, watching her eyeballs roll under the lids. Her breath rasps heavy off her throat as she sleeps.

Marlene used to be a force of nature! I suppose she always drank a little but not like this. She was sharp. I told her everything. She had it drilled into my head that once you catch a person in a lie, it's hard to ever trust that person again. By "person," she meant me. Us. Everyone else was gray area.

Sometimes she breaks my heart, though. In the middle of the night, after Nadia told her off, I woke up to my mother screaming. I jumped out of bed just as her

bedroom door flung open. She ran into the kitchen.

She pulled a butcher knife out of the sink. In just her bra and panties, she turned the point of the blade toward her stomach. Then she stopped and let it drop. "It's too dirty," she said, as she sank to the floor, choking on her tears. "And I'm too fat. It'll never go in. How did I get so fat?"

I tried to help her up, but she swiped at me to leave her alone. I thought about calling my dad. We hadn't heard from Sam in months. I wished he'd come here, sort of, but I didn't want him seeing her like this.

My mom is supposed to be beautiful and smart. That's the Marlene I want my dad thinking about. Not this Marlene, lying here, pale and lumpy and hating her own guts.

Back in her bed, her hands are up near her shoulders, gripping the edge of the sheet like a little girl in a Christmas story. The polish on her nails is chipped to hell, and one fingertip jumps, kicking out like a dying bug's leg. My mom's nail polish used to be perfect. You could see your reflection in those nails. The Lady Leni, my dad used to call her. He called her Leni when he loved her, short for Marlene. I was little then. We were all little, in my head.

━ ●

When I came home from school today, Marlene was out. No note, again. I mean, seriously, think about it. If I disappeared and didn't call or leave a note to say where I was, she would *tweak*! It's just her and me. Me and her. She used to *understand* that. She used to *always* leave notes.

I yanked open the fridge: nothing but condiments and milk. I hate being hungry and feeling all hostile at the same time— it's as though acid's gnawing at my guts while someone is simultaneously wringing them out like a wet dishrag.

The tap dripped. I raked my front teeth over my bottom lip. Maybe if I washed the

dishes it wouldn't be so goddamn depressing around here. Crunchy bits munched underfoot on the linoleum as I doused the whole mess with dish soap.

Marlene claims she's on the wagon again—no more booze since her night with Jack, the bog man. But she goes apeshit if I move to kiss her when she comes in the front door. She thinks I'm trying to smell her breath. I am.

After the dishes, I turned on the television halfway through that old Scorsese movie *Alice Doesn't Live Here Anymore,* with Ellen Burstyn. Marlene loves that movie. So do I. I guess we sort of relate to it, even

though Marlene and I have way more secrets than the mother and son in that show. We live on secrets like some people live on McDonalds. I wonder sometimes what those bitches at school would think if they knew about me. Like I said, I don't drink or smoke. I'm like my dad in that way. Sam says addicts are weak. But at school, they all figure this means I'm totally soft. This chick named Laura Morris actually shoulder-checked me in the hall the other day and called me a pussy. I didn't do anything about it, so maybe she's got a point.

Nobody at school knows anything about me. They don't know where I came from or how we make a living. I know loan

sharks for chrissake! I've seen a gun! Not that I'm all superior about it, but *they're* the pussies, those girls, not me. They're clueless.

I picked up the phone and called Fat Freddy. "Heya kid," said Freddy. "Na, I haven't seen your mother lately. I figured she was either workin' solo or lambin' it. Ha ha…" That's Fat Freddy for you. Totally old school. My dad kind of talks like that, too. Sam calls crooked guys "rounders" and regular guys "square johns." I was pretty old before I realized regular people don't talk that way.

"You all alone over there, Samantha?"

I stared at the TV. "My boyfriend's here," I told him.

"Uh oh! I won't tell if you don't!"

I'm not crazy about Freddy. He's unsavory as far as I'm concerned. Fat Freddy is a fence who used to work with Marlene and my dad back when we were a family. After Sam ended up in jail, Fat Freddy weaseled in close to Marlene. He actually called here a few weeks ago to ask if we'd seen Sam.

"He was in town," he said. "I thought sure he'd've called you!"

He knew damn well Sam never called us. He just wanted to rub it in, get even because

Marlene doesn't call him much anymore. Even though she and Freddy used to make pretty good coin together when they ran the Birthday Girl scam.

It worked like this. Marlene would sit down at a hotel bar. She'd order herself a drink and ask the bartender his name. Flashing some cash around ("Can you break a hundred?"), she'd say that it was her birthday. Then, like it was confidential information, she would tell him that her boyfriend let her pick out her own present, and she'd show off her new diamond bracelet. The bartender might say, "Whoa, what'd that run the poor bastard?" I loved that part! She took me with her a couple

of times when I was a little kid and it made my stomach flip-flop the way she would scrunch up her nose when she whispered, "*Six thousand, two hundred, and twenty-five dollars!*" Actually, she'd bought it for six bucks off some street vendor.

When she finished her drink, she'd gather up her things and surreptitiously drop the bracelet under the bar stool. A few minutes later, Fat Freddy (or my father, when I was a kid) would walk in and take the seat Marlene had just left. Not long after that, Marlene would phone the bar, all frantic. The bartender would look for the bracelet. Freddy would move his foot—"You mean this?"

But Freddy wouldn't hand the bracelet over, just eyeball it and whistle maybe. "Ask if there's a reward," he'd say.

On the phone, Marlene would cry. I watched her do it, watched her cradle the receiver as she pushed out tears, even though no one could see her. "I have to get that bracelet back. Please. Tell him I'll give him a thousand dollars. Cash." Nearly every time, the bartender would hang up and haggle. He'd offer Freddy fifty bucks, imagining he'd pocket the difference when Marlene showed up with a thousand.

Freddy would laugh. "Forget it, man." He'd hold onto the bracelet. "I gotta get goin'."

The bartender would get anxious then, and Freddy could usually get anywhere from two hundred to four hundred bucks out of him. One time, he and Marlene got five hundred!

Marlene said it wasn't stealing because if the bartender hadn't been such a lying, cheating dirtbag in the first place, he'd never have given the money to Freddy. I always wondered about that reasoning, though. What if the bartender wasn't looking to pocket the difference? What if he was just trying to help Marlene—the damsel in distress—get her bracelet back from the creepy guy who'd found it? She never went back to that bar again, so how could she know for sure?

Marlene and Freddy had a decent business partnership for a while, but it soured. Fat Freddy had a major crush on Marlene. Something happened—I don't know what, but Marlene made it clear that she wasn't into him and Freddy couldn't handle the rejection. That sort of thing screws up a lot of friendships. People don't want to pine for too long.

There was no food in the house and my stomach was making jungle noises. Turning off the TV, I hauled open the sliding glass doors and scissored my legs over the balcony railing. I don't like working close to home but sometimes you have to.

Outside the drugstore, I hung around the garbage can till I'd managed to fish out a few cash-register receipts. My dad taught me this one when I was a kid. You have to act normal, you can't make a big deal out of hunting for receipts or some uptight tool might notice and go squealing to a cop or something. The best one I found had a pregnancy test, mascara, foundation, lipstick, and blusher. Total: $63.50. *Nice.* For appearance's sake, I snagged an empty store bag that had blown against the outside wall.

Inside the store, I lifted the items off the shelves. Marlene would've freaked; she thinks shoplifting is totally low class.

The problem with this scam, though, is you have to be exact. I had almost everything—the same pregnancy test, mascara, foundation, and lipstick—and then I couldn't find the right blusher. *Shit!* I found the tag on the shelf but there was none left. I started to panic. But you can't panic or people notice.

"Can I help you find something?"

*Shit-shit!* It was one of those cosmetic-counter ladies, wearing a ton of makeup and fake pink nails.

"No. I mean, yeah. I'm trying to find this, um, stuff and they're all, umm—." Real smooth. What a loser.

"Oh, they didn't put those out yet," she said. "That shipment came in this morning. Can you wait just a moment?"

So I stood there and waited for her to bring me some blusher to steal. *God!*

Five minutes later, I chose the "English Suede" shade, thanked her with this big phony smile, and took off to another aisle. When I got the store bag out of my pocket, my chest was banging so hard, I thought I was going to have a heart attack. I was totally freaked and thinking I should put it all back. Maybe I *am* soft. I'm soft for a rounder that's for sure. My legs were all wonky and wooden. I made myself go to the checkout, though.

I dumped the pregnancy test and makeup on the counter and handed over the receipt. The cashier slapped down a pad of return slips. This is the *worst*—when you're freaking and you still have to close the deal. I took a deep breath, pulled my hands out of my pockets, and wrote down a fake last name and number. As she reversed the charges and I took the cash, I started thinking about how disgusted my dad would be by this lame performance of mine.

"Samantha!"

My head snapped around. It was Drew, two people behind me in line.

I froze a second. "Hey, how's it going?" I made a show of checking my watch as I headed for the door. "I've got to go to the supermarket for my mom."

"Wait." His woolly blond lion hair hid his face as he counted out change to pay for a pack of gum. He says he leaves his hair kind of long to distract from his big nose and his zits, but his skin's not that bad. And I like his nose. I felt melty inside for a second and then sort of ashamed and back to nervous.

"I'll wait for you outside." I wanted to get out of that store before a security guy's hand landed on my shoulder.

Drew came out a few seconds later, and we headed down the strip-mall sidewalk. The air between us was kind of clunky. We hadn't talked for two or three days. Because of a stupid argument. To be honest, I can't even remember what it was about. Marlene says I'd argue with my big toe if there was no one else in the room. *She* should talk.

"You going to the DYF roller party?" he asked me. His voice was tight and sort of worried sounding.

"Doubt it."

DYF stands for Divine Youth Fellowship —Tenth Avenue Divine is the name of

Drew's church. I went with him to a DYF roller party once. At the rink, I said "shit" and Mandy Peterson, one of the DYFers, looked at me like I'd just ripped off a big fart. "I used to swear," Mandy said to me. "People underestimated me when I swore."

"I called your place a couple nights ago," Drew told me now. "Your mom said you were at the movies."

Like I was going to stick around *there*? Forget it. After Nadia reamed out my mother, I got out of our apartment as soon as I could. The repertory theater was showing a couple of classics. "*Thelma and Louise* was playing at the rep. Double bill with *Butch Cassidy and the Sundance Kid.*"

Drew chewed at his nails as we walked. "You went by *yourself*?"

I shrugged. "I only stayed for *Thelma and Louise*. It's old but it's really cool. At the end, they drive straight off a cliff and it's like they're flying. It's like, for the first time in their lives, they're doing what they want."

"Don't start." His voice went hard. "I hate when you talk like that. They *died*, okay— don't make it all romantic. They had no respect for life."

"Just 'cuz they're girls, they're supposed to be lovey and sweet? Nobody thought it was terrible when Butch and Sundance went out in a hail of bullets."

"I thought you didn't stay for *Butch Cassidy*?" Drew stopped and stared at me. "Are you in trouble?"

I stopped, too. My chest went tight.

"A *pregnancy* test?" he whispered. He jammed his hands in his pockets. Drew's got room for ten hands in those pockets of his. Six foot one and I'd be surprised if he weighed 140 pounds.

"I was taking it *back*, dufus."

"Your face is red," he said. His was, too.

My mind bugged around for an explanation. I hate lying to Drew, but he asks too many damn questions.

"You're such a goof." I laughed. "My mom bought it by mistake. She thought it was a douche. Okay? She's a total zone-out." I started down the strip again.

Drew caught up with me. "Then why haven't you been returning my calls?"

"My dad was in town," I blurted. "I didn't call him back either."

Instantly, I wished I'd never said that. Then I couldn't shut up. "He was here for a week."

Drew trotted to keep up. "Why didn't you call him?"

"Because he didn't call me." I shoved my way through the supermarket door.

"What?"

I squinted at him. "My *dad* didn't *call* me."

At the mystery-meat section, I grabbed a package of hotdogs. I watched my feet on the supermarket linoleum as I walked to the bread aisle. Sappy music dribbled through the store. Drew scrambled along beside me.

"That's shitty, Sammie. I'm—I'm sorry. I thought you were pissed with *me*."

I snatched a bag of buns off the shelf and

started back toward the front of the store, my head ready to explode. I don't know what to do when I get like this. I don't know where to put it. "Laura Morris called me a pussy. And shoulder-checked me." My voice got loud. "Laura Morris doesn't even *know* me!"

"Jeez, Laura never—. Were you guys arguing?"

I stopped in the aisle and stared at him. "I never said thing-one to her!"

"You must've said *something*. I mean, to make her—"

My hand shot out and shoved him against

the preserves. His face was shocked as his head hit the shelf. A jam jar fell past his ear and busted open on the floor.

We both stared. It looked so horrible, the bloody red of it, like the inside of a skull. A big goose egg sat in my throat and I couldn't swallow.

Drew looked at me. His mouth opened. I left him standing there and took off for the cashiers.

See what I mean? I stand there yelling at Drew when it's Marlene who deserves it. It's *her* who deserves the beat-down. She

doesn't even try to act decent anymore.
Not to me. She doesn't act like we're a
team. Like Freddy said, she's workin' solo
these days.

Sitting on the edge of her bed now, I can
still see that jam jar, the red, brainy meat
of it lying beside Drew's foot. If my
mother had jumped off the roof the other
night the way she'd promised, I guess her
skull would have busted open just like that.

Her mouth is open now, her breath roaring
in and out, snoring off her throat. It seems
to be such an effort for her to just be to
just breathe and be alive. One of the times
she talked about knocking herself off, she

said that sometimes she can't bear waking up again, can't bear having to put in one more goddamn stinking day.

It sounds horrible, but I'm starting to think there won't be any peace around here till she gets her way. When I imagine stepping in front of a bus or swallowing every pill in her sacred bottle of Valium, it isn't the same. All I want is for it to be gentle around here. Calm.

That's the difference between Marlene and me. I don't mind the living part. I just want some peace and quiet. If you think about it that way, there's no point in me killing *myself*. She's the one who really

wants to go. I could be useful in all this. I could help.

━━ ●

By about eight o'clock, I still hadn't heard from Marlene. Not much chance she'd be working. She isn't that good alone—she's not a skilled planner. Anyway, she's been skittish since that hustle went bad a couple of years back. And that's another thing. That night probably would have come off if she hadn't got so cocky. The idea was to hang out in a casino bar and flirt with a high roller who'd just won big. If the sucker warmed up to her, she'd sneak

knockout drops into his drink. When he looked drowsy, she'd go up to his room with him, and as soon as he passed out, she'd go through his wallet. And then she'd get the hell out of there.

But this guy woke up too soon. He knocked her around pretty bad. It was after that that we had to go on Welfare. I don't blame her. Yes I do—it was a bullshit con. She shouldn't have gone into any sucker's room. She ended up in the hospital for chrissake. And then on painkillers. And tranquillizers. And then vodka with tranquillizers, until she couldn't get through a day without them.

My stomach churned again—those hard hands wringing my guts. I wondered if Marlene had her car. It freaks me out when she drives now.

I finished my last hotdog and went downstairs to check.

The cool cement of the underground parking sent a jolt up my bare feet into my shinbones. The slap of each step echoed around the walls. I glanced over my shoulder, thinking about all the horrible rape stories that take place in underground parking lots—and then slammed face first into George, the caretaker.

"Hello, Sammie," he said.

Up close like that, George is enormous, a wall.

"What's this?" He swiped a finger across my chin and then smelled it. Showing me a smear of mustard, he said, "You should stay away from that junk food."
I caught his wink through those tinted glasses he wears, and I moved away a step.

"And what are you doing with bare feet, you little rascal?" He reached out and slapped my butt.

A stupid laugh came out of me and I wanted to punch myself for it. I skittered

away toward Marlene's parking stall. "Just, ah, wanted to get something out of the car."

"Sammie, you give any more thought about the class?" George's voice echoed.

The stall was empty. "*Shit.* She's driving," I muttered and started back.

He walked alongside me. "I told you that I'm coaching the drama?" His eyebrows formed an A-frame over his glasses. Yeah, he'd told me—about a hundred times. George complains that he used to coach great theater actresses in Romania, but here all anyone wants to do is get acting jobs on crappy TV shows. If he's so great,

though, what's he doing managing *this* dump?

"I'm thinking about it."

"Don't waste time thinking...," he said, as he plucked my wrist through the air like a coin from an ear. "You got something." My hand was sandwiched between both of his now. "I know what I'm talking about. You have great potential."

"Ha ha," I said again and pulled my hand back. I felt nervous, like Marlene would be pissed with me for not telling him to eff off. But I wasn't sure if he had technically done anything that bad. Plus, there's the

fact that George was the only thing between us and the street.

I reached the door and jammed my key in the lock. "I'll ask my mom."

"We can work something out," he said, pulling the door open for us.

Inside, he poked the elevator call button and then patted my shoulder with a heavy thump. "We'll work it out, Sammie-girl."

When the doors opened, George paused with his "ladies first" gesture. The idea of getting into a steel box with him suddenly made me queasy.

"Actually," I said, "I'm gonna take the stairs. Gotta check the mail."

Back in the apartment, I had a black-cloud kind of feeling, and I couldn't shake it. I got out the White Pages and flipped chunks of gray leaf, searching for a number. It was almost nine o'clock now.

When I got the nearest hospital on the line, I asked if someone by my mother's name had come into Emergency. Nope. I hung up and dialed the downtown general hospital. "You don't have a Marlene Bell admitted there, do you?"

They didn't.

I hung up and stared into space.

She swore she was off the booze.

I went into her bedroom. Her bed was made at least. She hardly ever makes her bed when she's on a bender. I was about to leave but something made me look in her closet instead. Some dresses were heaped on the floor in a suspicious kind of jumble. I got down and pulled them aside: a jug of red wine sat there, half empty.

My fists slammed into my thighs. "*Liar!*" I pulled it out of the closet into the light. Unscrewing the cap, I sat over it and the sour-fruit smell hit me.

"*Stupid, lying*—" Suddenly I had the jug in both hands, tilted toward my mouth. The wine sloshed onto my chin as I guzzled.

"How do *you* like it?" I said, dropping the bottle and letting the rest chug onto the rug. Up off the floor, I yanked open her top drawer. Empty pill bottles rolled around, but I found one still full of Valium and pulled off the lid. Before I could think, I'd dumped them into my mouth.

Breath puffing through my nose, cheeks full of pills, I stood there blinking out tears. I gagged, opened my mouth, and let the pills drop into her drawer. Some stuck to my tongue and the insides of my cheeks with

the taste of something dead and rotten, and I had to use my finger to peel them out. Tears were sliding and stinging now. I left the pills where they lay and went into the bathroom to rinse my mouth.

"Everything's because of you!" I screamed back at her bedroom. "You should drop dead, not me!" My hands were shaking. I hate when I cry over her. I hate it. I wished she'd just die, and I was scared that she might.

In the living room, I dug into the phone book again. I picked up the phone and dialed the main police station downtown. My jaw shook and I was afraid I couldn't talk right.

A man answered, Sergeant Somebody.

I hung up.

If she got hurt, who'd call me? If she got busted, who'd call me?

I redialed. "You didn't come across a woman named Marlene Bell tonight, did you?"

"Bell? Lemme have a look... No." The cop let out a stilted sort of chortle. "Should we be expecting her?"

"No. She's—she should be home and I thought...an accident, maybe."

Silence on his end, and then, "Okay, why

don't I call you back if I hear anything?
Who knows, eh?" He read my number
back from his call display.

Stupid, I thought. I'm so *stupid*! Heat ran
up and down my arms and I wondered if it
was the wine. Booze gives Marlene the
guts to do whatever the hell she wants. I'm
not Marlene. The cop had my number.
Probably even knew where I lived. I mumbled yes and hung up.

Wrapping my arms around my knees, I
sat, squeezing them. What if she did die,
I thought. Then what? I took a big breath
and stared toward the dark windows. I'm
the one who takes care of everything

around here anyway. The thing is, you can't just sit around and wait for bad shit to happen. You have to plan ahead and take care of yourself.

Planting my feet back on the floor, I decided it was time to get practical. Why put off the inevitable? I'd pretend Marlene was already dead. First off, I'd need money—I'd have to cash our welfare check. If I was smart, I could deposit it and then write myself a personal check from Marlene.

Some of Marlene's canceled checks sat halfway out of a bank envelope on the coffee table. I opened and closed my hands. I sat up straight before I reached for one.

Laying a piece of paper over her signature, I traced it once. Then again. After a few more tries, I did it freehand. The phone rang and I jumped.

"Sammie?" It was Drew. "What the hell is wrong with you?"

"Nothing," I snapped. "I'm just—*nothing*." I crumpled up the signatures.

"You nearly split my friggin' head open!"

There was a long silence. "I'm sorry."

"Well—? What the hell?"

"I said I was sorry. I'm—I'm just stressed.

Your little honey Laura Morris shoving me around..." Why couldn't he have just pushed me back at the supermarket, just given me a good smack? But he would never do that. I shouldn't even have a friend like Drew. Drew is going to heaven. Me and Marlene are not.

"*Honey*? Not *my* honey. Anyone who shoves people around is no friend of mine. Unless it involves a fruit preserve."

Even when I've been a total bag, he finds a way to make me laugh.

"How's your mom?" he asked all of a sudden.

"Why?"

"Cuz I called the other night. When you were out watching Thelma and Louise drop off a cliff. Your mom was really funny.... She thought someone had broken into the apartment and kept saying, '*Who's there?*' in this man-voice. She put the phone down a minute and went to check and then she came back on the line and said she had a hammer for protection." He giggled.

I wanted him to just shut up and be near, to hold a tip of me, just the cuff of my shirt. My pinky.

"She kept saying, 'I need a man!' She wanted me to come over. She's like—"

"Here? She wanted you to come *here*?"

"She'd just had a few. She didn't mean anything."

"Shut up."

He had to be bullshitting. Maybe this was Drew hitting back, finally.

There was another long silence, then, "I read a poem to her. It's—I wrote it for you."

"She's had *loads* of guys, you know. What does she need with some zit-faced dork?"

"Samantha, don't be shitty. I shouldn't have told you. I'm sorry. Look, can I just—

can I read it? I need to tell you..." He went quiet again. Then he murmured something else, and I felt my chest caving in when he said it. I wanted to punch Marlene and him and the mirrors and the walls. But I just sat there, sucking inside-out instead.

"I love you," he said again.

Like getting my head held under water. Like a pillow pressed over my face.

I hung up.

It was five after ten when the phone rang again. I didn't want to talk to him. Anyone who says *I love you* is just holding you hostage. Drew should drop dead. He

should take it back. I snatched the phone out of the cradle.

It was the cop, Sergeant Whatshisname. "Did someone from this number call about a woman named Marlene Bell? Well, we got her here now."

"Is she okay?"

"Seems okay."

"Will she lose her driver's license?"

"She wasn't driving. We found her wandering around Broadway and Main. If you want to come get her—actually, we'll hang on to her for a couple more hours, let her

sober up. You can come any time after midnight. You driving?"

"I don't have my license yet," I mumbled. "I just turned sixteen."

His silence was the worst part. "Do you have someone you can call?" he finally asked. "And bring her some clothes."

"Clothes?"

"She was wearing a sleeping bag and one clog when we picked her up. Come by any time after midnight." He rattled off the address.

It was dead quiet after I hung up. Now

what? See, this is how Marlene pushes me against the wall. She fucks up and I have to fix it. I can't fix every goddamn mistake she makes! Who do you call when your *mother*'s in jail? How totally screwed is that?

I stared at the phone. Who? Freddy? Some fat old fence who wants to grope everything he gets near?

My dad? I don't even know where Sam is.

Who do I have?

I have Drew. I *had* Drew. Before he had to go and wreck it with that I-love-you crap. I felt like I was going to start bawling again. Because Drew is the only one. He's the only one in the world who gives a shit.

I picked up the phone.

Drew's mother answered. "It's after ten, Samantha." Her voice was suspicious and tinny. Drew's mother's got my number alright. Drew told me that she said I was a bad apple. She called her son now and told him to be quick about it.

"Samantha?" His voice was strained and huffing, like he'd been holding his breath. "I'm sorry," he whispered. "I just meant like a friend. You're my best friend. Like that, okay? I love you like that."

I kept swallowing and looking at the clock. After midnight, the cop said. How could Drew help me after midnight? And

how could he love me if he knew what my family was really like?

━━ •

It was quarter to one when I got into Drew's dad's car. He'd told me we'd meet at quarter after twelve. "What took you so long?"
"You think he just handed me the keys?"

"Sorry."

"My dad'll shit a brick if he catches me. What's in the bag?"

"Nothing." I scrunched the plastic in my lap. "Clothes. Can we go?"

Drew peered past the steering wheel and carefully put the car into Drive. Streetlights illuminated the hard, red bumps on his skin, turning them purple in the night. He was so embarrassed about his zits. In this light, they made him look wounded and I hated myself for calling him a zit-faced dork. I wished we could be quiet and hug for a long time. Instead, we eased forward, Drew's hands firmly at ten and two o'clock on the wheel.

As we got closer to the station, the streets got grimier and lonelier—as if the whole neighborhood served you right for being a screw-up.

It was half past one when we found the place: a big, ugly brick building with small, caged windows lit yellow. Drew turned off the ignition.

"I can't do this," I blurted.

He looked at me. "You want me to go? I'll go."

I nodded and handed him the bag of clothes. He handed me the car key. "In case you want to listen to the radio or something." He got out.

He blinked up at the police station a moment. I watched his skinny legs, lost in the bag of his jeans, as he went up the concrete steps.

Once he disappeared, I stared at the dashboard and listened to the engine click as it
cooled.

*"I'll kill you!"* somcone yelled. I twisted
around to see two guys staggering down
the block. One threw a fist into the other
guy's chest and sent him sprawling. These
two ass clowns were loose and Marlene
was behind bars. In the movies, they always
make it look all adorable when some chick
is drunk off her butt. But in real life, people
hate her, they want to make her disappear.

I pushed the remote on the key and all the
doors locked.

Eventually they came out, Drew with a
red-plaid sleeping bag under one arm and
my mother's elbow in his opposite hand.
Marlene pulled free, leaned on the banister,
and slid the rest of the way down. She
stumbled off the last step and Drew
caught her elbow again.

Giggling, she squealed, "You are my
prince," and grabbed Drew's face.

"Shut up," I said to the dashboard.

"God, you're *cute*!" she yelled at him.

Drew kept a hand across her back and brought
her over to the passenger side. I shoved my
door open. Marlene's face lit up as I got out.

Reading my eyes, she said, "Oops. I'm in trouble. My little girl thinks I'm a *loo-hoo-hooser*." She made an L out of her thumb and finger and planted it on her forehead.

I got into the back seat. I wanted her up front, not sitting behind me, playing with my hair or trying to maul me.

After Drew closed the passenger door, Marlene turned around in her seat and looked at me. "He's a *doll*," she said. "You should marry him." She blinked and then reached for my face. "Look how pretty you are…my angel. You're my sweet angel." She went suddenly serious. "If it weren't for you, I'd be dead, you know."

My mother's fingers kept reaching, and so I leaned forward, took hold of them, and pressed them to my cheek. Her eyes welled up until tears dribbled down.

You'd think, after everything, that Marlene would have given up hustling and drinking. That she'd have gotten religion—joined a choir! Instead, it's me nosing around the church pews hunting for someplace quiet.

It's past three in the morning now. Drew drove home with his dad's car. For a guy who's in church every Sunday, Drew's dad seems pretty mean. I wonder what he'll do if he finds out.

"Everything's going to be okay," Drew
kept telling me. He said he wished I could
come stay with him, sleep in his brother's
old bed. "I'm going to ask my mom, okay?
Don't you have, like, a social worker-type
person? Cuz of The Welfare?"

"No! I mean, yeah. Some chick came
nosing around last year to make sure
we weren't rich. I'm not calling *her*."

 "Maybe you should," Drew said. "I'm
scared that if you don't—."

"The caretaker thinks I should be an
actress," I said.

 "He's a creep." His eyes flicked away. "I'll

talk to my mom. She…" Drew stuttered
till his words went straight again. "I won't
let anything happen to you."

I could feel myself starting to bawl, so I
made him go.

I am sitting on the edge of Marlene's bed
now, with a pillow in my fists. Watching
her eyelids twitch.

When we got home from the cop station,
I found one of those Valium that I'd spat
into her drawer and handed it to her with
a glass of water. I asked her how she ended
up on Broadway wearing a sleeping bag.
She was with a guy, she said, and then
shrugged.

I lean in now while she breathes all raspy
and I inhale, as if swapping our breath
might let me see into that skull of hers, see
her night projected like a home movie.

I don't know what's true about us anymore.
I'm scared we're just bad, right through.

Sitting back, I grip the feather pillow in my
lap. I stare at her for a few more seconds.

I raise the pillow, square it just above her
face, and imagine setting it down, keeping
the feathers loose so that the puffy bits get
sucked into her nose and mouth when she
tries to breathe.

I feel sick inside and take the pillow back.

I don't know if I mean it, what I'm thinking of doing.

Yes, I do. I mean it. She wants this. I'm only helping.

I set it light against her face. I hold it there.

At first nothing happens. Then her hands twitch and come up to grope the air. Her voice echoes in my head again: *If it weren't for you, I'd be dead.* A flash of her bleeding face comes to me, her scared eyes—crying, on her hands and knees in that hotel corridor, while the guy she'd tried to hustle screamed "thief" and "whore." Security guards kept him pinned to the wall. That was two years ago last month.

My hands push the pillow in against her face. *If it weren't for you, I'd be dead.* Her breath crackles and goes quiet.

I snatch the pillow off and stare. Her face is slack.

Then her eyes blink open. "What's the matter?" Her voice is hoarse. She glances at the door, like she's scared. "Where's Sammie?"

"I'm right here."

"No." She shakes her head. "Little Sammie." She does that sometimes when she's half asleep or messed up—forgets I'm not a little kid anymore. She closes her eyes now and drifts.

I look at her and shiver. What a life-giver
I am. What a sweet creep of a grave robber.
Chucking the pillow on the rug, I flow
like a nasty black river down the hall.

I know she loves me. I love her, too. I do.

My throat is squeezing shut and I can't
breathe so great.

In the living room, I sit on the couch and
drag in some air. I can't imagine a social
worker is going to give a damn about me.
Not really. Maybe she would.

Then there's George and his drama
classes. "You have great potential," George
tells me again.

"I won't let anything happen to you," Drew says.

Marlene is whispering in there, too—*If it weren't for you.*

Just shut up, all of you. I need quiet. I have to think. I will make my way out of this. Just give me some quiet. There is a way out.

I pull my knees up, rest my head against them, and breathe.

Single Voice
Single Voice

Single Voice